Panda Bear's PAINTBOX

By Michaela Muntean

Illustrated by
Christopher Santoro

A GOLDEN BOOK, NEW YORK
Western Publishing Company, Inc., Racine, Wisconsin 53404

Text copyright © 1981 by Western Publishing Company, Inc. Illustrations copyright © 1981 by Christopher Santoro. All rights reserved. Printed in the U.S.A No part of this book may be reproduced or copied in any form without written permission from the publisher. GOLDEN®, GOLDEN & DESIGN®, A FIRST LITTLE GOLDEN BOOK®, and A GOLDEN BOOK® are trademarks of Western Publishing Company, Inc. Library of Congress Catalog Card Number: 80-85085 ISBN 0-307-10105-3/ISBN 0-307-68105-X (lib. bdg.)
KLMNOPQRST

S0-BTZ-056

Panda Bear's daddy gave him a paintbox. It was a wonderful paintbox, with a long skinny space for the brush and a row of little squares filled with different colors. Panda Bear thought they looked like little windows.

"I will paint a picture right now," Panda Bear said. "And the picture I paint will be a picture of me."

First he painted his head and tummy white.
Then he painted his ears, nose, eyes, arms,
and legs black.

Panda Bear looked at his picture. "I look too plain in black and white," he said. "I will paint myself a red scarf."

So Panda Bear painted a long red scarf
around his neck. It reached all the way across
the paper. "My long red scarf is blowing in
the wind," he said.

Then he painted a bright blue sky. "Even though it is windy," he said, "the sky is blue and the sun is shining." He painted a big yellow sun in the bright blue sky.

Then something strange happened.

Some of the blue sky got mixed with the yellow sun. Panda Bear was very surprised. "Blue and yellow make *green!*" he cried.

"I will paint some green grass in my picture," Panda Bear said, "to show that on this sunny, windy day spring is on the way."

After Panda Bear painted some patches of green grass, he looked at his picture and thought, "If yellow and blue make green, I wonder what yellow and red make."

So he mixed some yellow and red.
They made orange!

"Orange is just the right color for a pair
of mittens," Panda Bear said.

"Even though the sun is shining and spring is on the way, the wind is blowing, and I will need a pair of mittens."

Panda Bear wasn't finished painting yet.
"If red and yellow make orange," he thought,
"what will red and blue make?"

He mixed red and blue. They made purple!
"Purple," said Panda Bear, "is a fine color
for a pair of boots."

"I look very nice," he thought when he
was finished, "but I look lonely all by myself.
I will paint my friend Brown Bear standing
next to me."

"Brown Bear likes the color pink," said Panda Bear. So he mixed white and red and painted Brown Bear a fuzzy pink hat to keep his ears warm.

Just as Panda Bear finished, his mother walked in. She looked at the picture and she looked at Panda Bear. "Oh, Panda," she said, "there is red paint all over your elbow!"

"That is the color of my red scarf
blowing in the wind," Panda Bear said.

"And there is orange paint on your nose,"
his mother sighed.
"That is the color of my mittens,"
Panda Bear said.

"And there is blue and yellow and green and purple and brown and pink paint all over you!"

"Those are the colors of the sky and the sun and the grass and my boots and my friend Brown Bear with his pink hat on to keep his ears warm."

"I know," said his mother, "but that's too many colors for a Panda Bear."

And quicker than you can say "Panda Bear needs a bath" he found himself in a warm, soapy tub.

Panda Bear watched the colors mix with the soapsuds and then go swirling down the drain:

But he knew where he could find them all again — in his wonderful paintbox with the long skinny space for the brush and the little squares that looked like tiny windows filled with different colors.